Voices From Scotland

Edited By Holly Sheppard

First published in Great Britain in 2019 by:

Young Writers
Remus House
Coltsfoot Drive
Peterborough
PE2 9BF
Telephone: 01733 890066
Website: www.youngwriters.co.uk

Foreword

Dear Reader,

You will never guess what I did today! Shall I tell you? Some primary school pupils wrote some diary entries and I got to read them, and they were **excellent!**

They wrote them in school and sent them to us here at Young Writers. We'd given their teachers some bright and funky worksheets to fill in, and some fun and fabulous (and free) resources to help spark ideas and get inspiration flowing.

And it clearly worked because **WOW!!** I can't believe the adventures I've been reading about. Real people, make believe people, dogs and unicorns, even objects like pencils all feature and these diaries all have one thing in common – they are **jam-packed** with imagination!

We live and breathe creativity here at Young Writers – it gives us life! We want to pass our love of the written word onto the next generation and what better way to do that than to celebrate their writing by publishing it in a book!

It sets their work free from homework books and notepads and puts it where it deserves to be – **out in the world!** Each awesome author in this book should be **super proud** of themselves, and now they've got proof of their imagination, their ideas and their creativity in black and white, to look back on in years to come!

Now that I've read all these diaries, I've somehow got to pick some winners! Oh my gosh it's going to be difficult to choose, but I'm going to have **so much fun** doing it!

Bye!

Holly

Contents

Kinross Primary School, Kinross

Benjamin Euan Gibb (7)	49
Cameron Wilson (7)	50
Ruby Lewis (7)	51
Thea Blackburn (7)	52
Isla Clemie (7)	53
Fraser Younie (7)	54
Esther-Joy Lois Johnston (7)	55
CJay Duncan (7)	56
Jamie Allan (7)	57
Douglas Brown (7)	58
Angus Younie (7)	59
Aaron George Yates (7)	60

Lasswade Primary School, Bonnyrigg

Marley Hunter (6)	61
Sophie Marsland (6)	62
Harris McGregor (7)	63
Brodie Ella Wilson (6)	64
Ellie Maxwell (6)	65
Elle Marion Toulouse (6)	66
Micheal Dougan (6)	67
Emma Stables (6)	68
Laila Heatlie (6)	69
Toby Briggs (6)	70
Jamie Hamlyn (6)	71
Benjamin Harris (6)	72
Maia Patricia Virgo (7)	73
Morven Thompson (6)	74
Poppy Ann Dunham (6)	75
Simrit Janjua (6)	76
Taylor McInnes (6)	77
Harris McKenzie (7)	78
Rhys Gladstone (7)	79
Lailah Wilson (6)	80
Faith Barker (6)	81
Emerson Milne (7)	82
Cameron Smith (6)	83
Eddie Price (7)	84
Mila Dickson (6)	85
Yolanda Lange (6)	86

Cohen Donoghue (6)	87
Harry MacGregor (6)	88
Keeley McKenna (6)	89
Carter Dewar (6)	90
Zaynab Wahid (6)	91
Aaliyah Milliken (6)	92
Riley Henry (6)	93
Megan Murphy (7)	94

Milton Of Leys Primary School, Milton Of Leys

Emily Grace Williamson (7)	95
Brooke McMillan (7)	96

St Pius X RC Primary School, Dundee

Michalina Slusarek (7)	97
Daniel Cecil (7)	98
Max Adam (7)	100
Gabriela Lesiecka (7)	102
Kevin Souter (9)	103

St Thomas' Primary School, Riddrie

Laura Kacala (6)	104
Findlay Smith (7)	105
Haifa Minhas (7)	106
Hayley-Jay Johnston (7)	107
Jessica Reilly (7)	108
Lewis Murray (7)	109
Hollie Sneddon (7)	110
Harlyn Jenkins (7)	111
Taylor-Anne Shreenan (7)	112
Gabriela Skolarczyk (6)	113

St Thomas' RC Primary School, Arbroath

Oliver Parker (7)	114
Nina Kosznik (7) & Lola Susan Heenan (6)	115
Connor Falconer (7)	116

Marty Emery (6)   117
Luca Cassidy (7)   118

Woodlands Primary School, Cumbernauld

Emily Elizabeth Doctor (7)   119
Lola McLean (8)   120
Poppy Millar (7)   122
Sonny Sandhu (7)   124
Lilly McLay (7)   125
Isla (7)   126
Tyler Rolland (7)   127
Lily-Anne Elizabeth Fraser (7)   128
Nathan Andrew Snedden (7)   129
Alannah Dyce (7)   130
Noah Meppem (7)   131

The Diaries

Dear Diary

Last year, after school, my dad came to pick me up because I was going to a lovely, good hotel for the night! Then I went to sleep in the dark night.

In the morning, I got ready in my sparkly dress and I went to the lovely cafe. Yummy. Then we went to the wildlife park! First, we saw the lions. We saw an amazing, big, big, big lion. Next, we went to see the tall giraffes. It was so big! Wow. Then we saw the elephant, a big, strong elephant. Then we went to see the lemur. He was climbing a tree. Then I wanted to see the tiger! We only saw one. I was sad. Dad said it was fast. I said, "Okay, thank you, Dad." Rowan wanted to see the penguins. One came out of its house.

Willow Bews (7)

Ardross Primary School, Ardross

Dear Diary

It was the school's spring fair and I bought a sparkly mitten from my teacher. My favourite part was the Creme Egg cupcake and inside it was half of a Creme Egg which was super good! After that, I went to my drama class. I only got to do one class because people were playing at Inverness. I saw my uncle and auntie Rachel, Flora and Seamus and when it finished, we went to the cinema to watch 'Dumbo'. I was so sad. My favourite part was when they let the baby elephant free. It was called Dumbo. On the way home, we were talking about it and then when we got there, we had dinner and we went to bed.

Alicia Morera (7)
Ardross Primary School, Ardross

Dear Diary

A couple of days ago I went horse riding with my granny and my mum. It was very sunny. My horse, Dory, is black and white and I was riding her. My granny was riding her horse. Polly is black and white as well. Once we tacked up the horses, we set off. I was scared because we had to go up a steep hill but I managed to get up it! After that, I went through places with lots of houses.

On the way home, I went to my granny's house and I played on my Wii with my uncle. When I got home, I had to play with my little brother. After that, Mikey went out hunting for foxes. Then I had dinner.

Kaitlin Geddes (7)
Ardross Primary School, Ardross

Dear Diary

I went to the doctor's and I went to the waiting room for the doctor to call my name. I was reading a cool comic book until the doctor called me to come. We came from the room and then the doctor asked me some questions about what was wrong. I said my head was hurting. The doctor told me to get up on the bed and then I got told to get off. I got off and they went to go and get some help.

Austin Stevenson (7)
Ardross Primary School, Ardross

Dear Diary

I went to the spring fair. I walked in and wow! There were thousands of things. First, I had an ice cream with strawberry sauce. Then I bought some things. I bought a watch for my mum. I bought plasticine and a magnet. I really loved the spring fair.

Jamie Smyth (6)

Ardross Primary School, Ardross

Dear Diary

I went on a plane with my dad to visit my grandparents in Spain. The huge plane flew through the air very quickly. We landed safely at the airport early in the morning. It was very windy.

Alberto Morera (5)

Ardross Primary School, Ardross

Dear Diary

I am at home at the dinner table building my Lego mansion from Marvel's Avengers Infinity War. I am still building it. It looks old and messy.

Logan Sutherland (7)
Ardross Primary School, Ardross

Dear Diary

I went to my dad's friend Kyle's house near Inverness. I like going there as I get to feed the sheep. I get to ride on Kyle's buggy.

Flynn Hull (5)

Ardross Primary School, Ardross

Dear Diary

Yesterday it was World Book Day. We came to school dressed up. I was a cartoon cricketer and it was fun! Then we made little aliens because we read the book! After, we got reading partners. Then we went to the grand opening for the school library. Then we had me time. It was the best day ever!

Ryan Hodgkins (6)
Barmulloch Primary School, Glasgow

Dear Diary

Yesterday it was World Book Day. We came to school dressed up. I was a princess. First, we went to the new, awesome library and it was good fun. Then we made colourful aliens with shapes and underpants.

Pearl Amarachi Okonkwo (5)

Barmulloch Primary School, Glasgow

Dear Diary

Yesterday it was World Book Day. First, we went to the school library. I was dressed up in my pyjamas. Then we made aliens. Next, we got reading buddies and we did drama. It was really, really good fun!

Bethany MacLeod (7)

Barmulloch Primary School, Glasgow

Dear Diary

Yesterday it was World Book Day. We came to school dressed up but I did not dress up. We made creepy aliens and after, we went with our reading buddies. Then we did some handwriting.

Jack Woodside (6)

Barmulloch Primary School, Glasgow

Dear Diary

Today I had the most amazing adventure ever. I was in the woods with my pet dinosaur, Dan. We were just walking and listening to the trees swishing and swirling when I saw a goblin guarding a secret tunnel! Dan jumped at him and he zoomed away like a bolt of lightning. Luckily, the entrance was open so we slid through it and when we got out, there was a troll just standing, waiting for someone or something. Just then, we tried to zoom past but the troll kicked a tree and blocked our path! I jumped on Dan's back and we ran. Dan pounced at the troll and he ran away. In the end, we went home and had some hot chocolate and that was the end of our amazing adventure.

Quinn Soames (7)
Bunessan Primary School, Bunessan

Dear Diary

Today I had the most amazing day. Me and my dragon went to the zoo and it was a huge surprise for me and my dragon. We weren't very patient but when we got there, I didn't know which animal to go and see first. Then I saw a cat and a dog! The cat and the dog were confused because they never knew dragons existed! I asked them if they wanted to live with me. They said yes. We were running out of time to see all the animals so we climbed onto the dragon's back so we could see all the animals!
In the end, we flew home and my dragon cooked hot dogs and marshmallows with his fire breath!

Ciara Elizabeth Cameron (7)
Bunessan Primary School, Bunessan

Dear Diary

Yesterday I went to a gymnastics competition with my family. When we got there, I got a mermaid slush and then I had a drink. It was so so cold and I got a bar of chocolate with it. Then everyone went in and lined up to do their gymnastics routines. My routine was forward roll, tuck jump, forward roll, straight jump, forward roll jump, half turn. That was practise! It was time to show the judges and then I saw where I came. I came first place! I was so happy! Then after, we got a chocolate cake and it tasted delicious. Then we went home. When I got home, I had my lunch and then I went straight to bed.

Macie MacLellan (6)
Easterfield Primary School, Fortrie

Dear Diary

Today I went to the funfair and I went with my mum, my dad, my brother and my sister. We paid for tickets and we went on the wheel. We went on the rocking horse and we went to have dinner. Then we went to the soft play. Then we were playing with my brother and my sister! We had supper and we slept in the car.

Shannade Cowie (6)
Easterfield Primary School, Fortrie

Dear Diary

We went to the zoo in Mum's car. My unicorn was in the boot. I felt a bit scared in case the animals chased me. We saw the penguin pool. My unicorn jumped into the water. They all played together. My unicorn turned the water rainbow coloured! It was amazing.

Alisha Cowie (5)
Easterfield Primary School, Fortrie

Dear Diary

I went to the zoo on Monday. Lola, my dog, came with me. I was happy. We saw a giraffe. Lola jumped in and chased the tall giraffe! The giraffe stopped and Lola jumped over it and landed in a bin! Lola was covered in banana peels. It was funny.

Kaeden Graeme Paterson (7)
Easterfield Primary School, Fortrie

Dear Diary

I went to the park because there was a funfair. I was surprised. Mummy was feeling happy. I ate blue candyfloss. I saw horses going round the arena. We had a picnic watching the horses. It was special and yummy.

Skye Isabella Armstrong (5)

Easterfield Primary School, Fortrie

Dear Diary

Yesterday I went to the zoo with my mum. I was happy and excited. My dad was at home. I bought tickets. I saw the giraffes. I had orange juice. I went home.

Finn Barnes (7)

Easterfield Primary School, Fortrie

Dear Diary

I went to the zoo when I was on holiday. I went with my family. I was happy because I wanted to see the gorillas and the giraffes.

Finlay Pirie (5)

Easterfield Primary School, Fortrie

Dear Diary

This morning I took my dog on a walk. Suddenly, all I could see was a beautiful rainbow. It came from out of nowhere and it was very bright. I looked at my dog, George, and his fur was full of rainbow colours. As I looked around, I saw a pond and in the reflection, I could see I had a lovely rainbow-coloured dress on. I wondered where I was and how I got there. Then I heard it. The beautiful sound of a unicorn neighing! It did not sound like a normal horse, it was prettier and almost like singing. I stood very still and it slowly came over to me. I put my hand out and it let me clap it. It felt amazing. Its coat was like cotton wool, so soft. Then a tiny little fairy appeared in front of my eyes! "Hello!" she said. "I can grant you one wish."

I said, "I wish I could fly on the unicorn and find the pot of gold at the end of the rainbow."

With a flick of her wand, I was in the air flying on the unicorn! After a few minutes, we landed at the end of the rainbow. In the grass, I could see a bright glow. Then I saw the pot of gold! It had lots of shiny coins inside. Then I heard my mum shouting, "Wake up, Lily!" *Wow*, I thought. *That was just a dream!* I sighed. Oh well.
As I got out of bed, I felt something underneath my foot. I looked down and there was a shiny coin on the floor! I picked it up. So it was true! I knew it was.

Lily Rose Stewart (7)

Gargieston Primary School, Kilmarnock

Dear Diary

I imagine that you won't believe me but last week I played football with an alien!
The match was difficult but we won three-two! Anyway, it made me feel elated.
My best players were Paulo Dybala, Granit Xhaka, Danny Rose, David de Gea and me, Thomas Connor, because when my team was losing two-nil, I encouraged them and we magically won three-two! However, before the match started the alien was rubbish so I had to teach him some tricks, such as the drag back. It was my pleasure! Today I received a great, shocking letter. It said: 'Dear Thomas, would you like to come to the Alien World Cup?' I'd better take milkshakes and sweets for the journey!

Thomas Valentine Connor (7)
Gargieston Primary School, Kilmarnock

Dear Diary

One afternoon I went on HMS Defender (D36), which is a Royal Navy type forty-five destroyer. It was cool and fun; it has a radar that spins. When I was on the ship, I saw a helicopter and a missile. Then I was shown how to shoot a machine gun on the deck! Next, I saw a survival suit and visited the ship's hospital and operating room. We went into the wardroom where officers ate their meals. The table was set for eight. After that, we went into the ops room where we couldn't take any pictures. Then we went on deck and saw the *Defender* sign and the big gun at the front of the ship. I had a great, awesome, lovely time on D36.

Mark Wilson (7)
Gargieston Primary School, Kilmarnock

Dear Diary

I visited Culzean Castle with my dad. The castle was enormous! When we went inside, we saw some shiny suits of armour belonging to old knights. Behind a red curtain was a secret door that led to an old-fashioned room. I crept through the creaky door and discovered some gold and silver treasure! I heard something moving in the corner of the room. I was terrified. Then I heard my puppy, Chester, barking on the other side of the room! I was so happy to see him. We giggled and then all headed to the delicious ice cream parlour for a special treat on the way home.

Pippa Lee (6)
Gargieston Primary School, Kilmarnock

Dear Diary

Today was brilliant. You will never believe what happened to me. I went to the zoo. I saw a lion, jaguar, tiger, hippo, zebra and much more! I got to touch a penguin. Then I smelt a hot dog and a burger so I got a giant hot dog and chips. I heard a lion roaring and a gorilla punching his chest loudly! I noticed the lion had escaped and it was coming for me and my hot dog! I chucked my hot dog into the lion's cage. It ran for the hot dog! The park ranger closed the cage door and I was safe.

Freya Ahrens (7)
Gargieston Primary School, Kilmarnock

Dear Diary

I was walking my dog to the park. It is a magical dog.

At the park, we were playing tig. After we went to the park, I went to my friend's house with my dog. I had lots of fun at my friend's house.

After I went to my friend's house, I went ice skating, but I can't ice skate. I helped my friend ice skate so he didn't fall.

Erin Bissett (6)

Gargieston Primary School, Kilmarnock

Dear Diary

On Saturday I went to my brother's football game. It was rainy. My brother's team won and the other team lost. We were soaking but it was fun. We were happy that my brother's team won! We went back from football and we had rolls with sausages and bacon. Me and my sister had tomato sauce. We loved it.

Katie Malcolm (5)
Gargieston Primary School, Kilmarnock

Dear Diary

One day, I made a new friend. She was called Lucey. I played with Lucey. It was so much fun playing with Lucey!
The next morning, me and Lucey went to the park. I went on the slide. Lucey went on the swing. After that, me and Lucey went home and at home, we had ice cream. It was so much fun!

Alyia Shafique (6)
Gargieston Primary School, Kilmarnock

Dear Diary

In six sleeps, I am going to Florida with my mum, dad, gran, grandpa and my brother, Cameron. I am going on a plane. When I get there, I am going to jump in the pool. I am going to Magic Kingdom to see Peter Pan at the castle! I am excited to see all the characters.

Lewis Robertson (5)
Gargieston Primary School, Kilmarnock

Dear Diary

I went to the zoo with my monster friend. His name is Elit. He is green and spotty and little. At the zoo, I found a Pokémon! It was Pikachu! He smiled at me and wiggled his tail. My monster was happy. I had fun.

Jacob Alan Bradley (5)
Gargieston Primary School, Kilmarnock

Dear Diary

Today I saw an amazing play that you would love to see. It had fairies and a unicorn. It was spectacular and everything was so, so magical! When it was time to go, I was sure that I would be going back tomorrow.

Jasmine McPartland (7)

Gargieston Primary School, Kilmarnock

Dear Diary

I went to Blackpool and I met a unicorn. She danced with me in the Tower Ballroom. After that, we had an ice cream.

Hope White (5)
Gargieston Primary School, Kilmarnock

Dear Diary

I woke up excited to play, but when I looked out my window, it was raining! I felt miserable. My gran and I decided to jetpack to the moon.

When we landed, a strange alien came to say hello and handed us a smoothie each! Me and my gran looked at each other and decided to drink them, not knowing we would turn into big, crazy aliens! I was purple with big, yellow spots and she was blue with pink spots. It was very scary. We followed the other aliens to a party room where we ate hot dogs and danced! Granny even did the splits and a cartwheel! She was nearly as good as me, I thought. Anyway, we jetpacked home before bedtime and as soon as I got in, I went straight to bed.

The next morning, I woke up and looked in the mirror. Oh no, I was still an alien!

Darcie Moore (7)
Glencairn Primary School, Motherwell

Dear Diary

One day, I went to the beautiful beach. I saw a tail. It was my mermaid friend, Christeana! She gave me a special necklace. "The necklace will turn you into a mermaid whenever you want!" she said.

An hour later, I was in the big ocean. "I can't believe it!" I said. Then I noticed I spoke under the sea! "Oh!" I said. Then we played under the sea mermaid games. It was really fun. I really loved it. Then I heard a noise and my necklace glowed. That meant I had to go! Then I swam and swam up to the very top of the deep, blue, shiny ocean. I said, "Goodbye!" and gave her a hug and finally went home.

Mollie McKay (7)
Glencairn Primary School, Motherwell

Dear Diary

One snowy day, me and my best friend, Neve, were at a snowy field. We saw a snow-white leopard and we rode it into a secret tunnel! We saw a village. A little man came in and he said, "Hello! Can you please help me? Our village is being attacked by a big monster!"

We said, "Sure!"

We got the monster and put it in a big cage! "Thank you so much!" he said. "Since you got the monster, we award you with two teleporting staffs each!"

"Thank you!" we said. "Now we are going to teleport back home. Bye!"

We got back home. I had a fun day!

Olivia Kinnear (7)
Glencairn Primary School, Motherwell

Dear Diary

I went to the park on Thursday with my friends. We had lots of fun! The first crazy thing that happened was when Layla got stuck in the baby swing! The second crazy thing was when Sadie did a backflip on a swing. After that, Evie got us ice cream. Hannah also did the floss. Next, Darcie was hanging from the monkey bars. Then I fell asleep on a brown bench. Hannah woke me up by saying, "Boo!"
I woke up and I got us some sweets. We ate and ate until we were full! After eating, Darcie dropped her money in a muddy puddle. We had an amazing day at the park on Thursday! All of us had a crazy day!

Zoe Biggans (7)

Glencairn Primary School, Motherwell

Dear Diary

On Monday I went to the big beach with my family. We had so much fun on the big beach. I swam in the shiny blue water.
The next day, I went to the big beach again and we bought ice cream, then swam in the shiny blue water. I saw a beautiful mermaid! She had beautiful, shiny pearls on her tail. The mermaid said to me, "Do you want to play with me, little girl?"
"Yes please!" So we played some sea games. We played sea tig and sea hide-and-seek. It was time to go home. "Goodbye," I said.
"Goodbye," the mermaid said.
I had an excellent day!

Oliwia Brzeska (7)
Glencairn Primary School, Motherwell

Dear Diary

Yesterday I went to the beach with Layla, Darcie, Zoe, Sadie and Hannah. When we got there, we all got into our swimming costumes. Zoe had a banana swimming costume. Layla had a watermelon swimming costume. I had a strawberry bikini. Darcie had a melon bikini. When we were all ready, we went to the beach shop to get mermaid tails. They were pink, purple and blue. We got into the mermaid tails and started to swim in the sea. We saw six mermaids and we all became friends. We had a splash! Then it was time to go to Layla and Darcie's house. I had an amazing day with my friends.

Evie Carrick (7)
Glencairn Primary School, Motherwell

Dear Diary

I went to school with my friends called Hannah, Zoe and Megan. We played in the playground and we had so much fun. Then the bell went. We went inside the school. We did Maths and then it was playtime. We had snacks. I played with my friend, Hannah, and then the bell went. We went inside and then we did spelling and reading. We read a book called 'A Footballer Called Flip'. Then it was lunchtime. I had a ham sandwich. After lunch, we had gym, but it started to rain so we had to go inside. It was a hard day.

Sophie Galloway (7)
Glencairn Primary School, Motherwell

Dear Diary

One day, I went out to the zoo with my best friend. I was so excited. When I got there, I saw a big elephant! Then we went to have lunch. I got a hot dog and my best friend got a burger. I got a milkshake and so did my friend. Then we went into the sweet shop and I got a big bag of sweets! The sweets were very hard. I got some blue and pink sweets. They were very sweet.
At the end of my exciting trip, I went into the toyshop. I got a big elephant. Then I was so sad to go. I had a fun day.

Emma Irvine (7)
Glencairn Primary School, Motherwell

Dear Diary

One day, I went to the park and when I was climbing, I saw a monster. I asked him if he wanted to play tig and he said yes, so we played tig. We played rock, paper, scissors to see who would be the catcher first. The monster lost when we played rock, paper, scissors so he was the catcher! The monster lost! It was dinner time and for dinner we had pizza. It was really good. Then it was time for bed so we went to bed.
In the morning, for breakfast we had toast and I went to school.

Lewis Kane (7)
Glencairn Primary School, Motherwell

Dear Diary

One year ago, I went to the biggest park in the world. Then I saw a very green alien coming down the slide! It came to me and said, "Hi! Do you want to play with me?" Then my dad told me to leave it alone. Then I played on the climbing frame and I didn't listen to Dad. It started raining so I said bye. The next day, it hurt itself. I helped it. I gave it an ice pack! I went home with it. Then I gave it hot cocoa. I made it my roommate.

Julius Kipre (7)
Glencairn Primary School, Motherwell

Dear Diary

Yesterday I went to Unicorn Land. When I went for a walk in Unicorn Land, I found a magical unicorn! Her name was Rainbow. She was a nice pastel pink colour. Then we ate lots of vanilla ice cream. We were hyper after that. Then we made bright pink slime! After that, we had to play with the slime because it was super soft. When we were finished with the slime, we went to the largest theme park in Scotland! We had the best day of our lives.

Holly Sneddon (7)
Glencairn Primary School, Motherwell

Dear Diary

Yesterday I went to the funfair with my friend, Evie. At the funfair, Evie and I got pink, fluffy candyfloss. Then we went on a ginormous, scary, black ride and it went in a loop-the-loop! After that, we went to the toyshop. Evie and I got fluffy unicorn toys. Then Evie and I went to my house and played with my dog, Lexi. Then Evie said to me, "That was a crazy day!"

Layla Moore (7)

Glencairn Primary School, Motherwell

Dear Diary

One sunny day, me and my unicorn friend, Sparkles, went to the beach. We had a wee picnic and then went fishing with our big, shiny, black, girl sunglasses on. We then went to the fish shop and gave the fish to the man! Me and Sparkles had a sleepover. We both met our rubber friend and had a disco party! We also had a McDonald's and played Angry Birds.

Poppy Macrae Smith (7)
Glencairn Primary School, Motherwell

Dear Diary

Me and my best friend, Lucy, went to the big, huge cinema to see a cool movie called 'The Boy Who Would Be King'. After we left, me and Lucy bought some delicious popcorn. We went home in the car. Lucy wanted to come over to my house for a wee.
When it was time for Lucy to go home, we said, "Bye!" We had a wonderful day.

Neve Olivia Lynch (7)
Glencairn Primary School, Motherwell

Dear Diary

I was bored so I went to the park with my friends. We were playing hide-and-seek so I hid in the bush but when I looked in the bush, there was actually a secret tunnel! It was as long as a mountain. I went into the tunnel. In the tunnel, I saw a humungous treasure chest! There was a key for the treasure chest behind a rock, so I opened the treasure chest with the key. There was a rocket! It was packed with milkshakes and sweets. The door opened and it went on its countdown. Quickly, I went in. Five, four, three, two, one, blast off! I went to the moon. I looked at a bump on the moon and an alien popped out! Then hundreds popped out! They tried to attack me but sea monsters protected me. I had a water gun and shot the king alien. They all died and I went home!

Benjamin Euan Gibb (7)
Kinross Primary School, Kinross

Dear Diary

So I was playing football in my garden like normal and my mum called me and she told me we were going to the shop. I brought my football.

When we got there, it was as cold as ice! My mum said that she would stay in the car so I went into the shop and got some fish. When they were getting me my fish, I found a secret hatch so I went in. All of the walls were chocolate! I walked some more and found gold and diamonds! I grabbed it all and tried to turn back but the hatch had sealed! I had to find another way out. I looked everywhere and eventually, I looked under the chest and found a hatch! I went down it and found a ladder that led back up. I went back to the car with our gold and diamonds!

Cameron Wilson (7)
Kinross Primary School, Kinross

Dear Diary

Guess what? I went to the funfair and just when I stepped in, I saw that it was the best thing ever. It was a unicorn! Me and the unicorn ran round and round until we found a fairy. Me, the unicorn and the fairy had a party! We had sweets and games and sweets and games. Then me and the fairy went on top of the unicorn and we flew to Unicorn Land and Fairy Land! Something was wrong. The other unicorns were not partying! When they saw us partying, they partied too, so they lived happily ever after!

Ruby Lewis (7)
Kinross Primary School, Kinross

Dear Diary

Once, I went horse riding and my horse was called Bear. My brother's horse was called Jas. My other brother's horse was called Molly. Bear's foot slipped but we were okay. Then we went past a park. Bear was as tall as a mountain and my head smacked against a branch! Then we went up the steep hill again but Bear was okay this time. Then we went back to the stables. I was sad to go home but it was worth it because we went back to the campsite. We had so much fun going horse riding!

Thea Blackburn (7)

Kinross Primary School, Kinross

Dear Diary

Once, I went to school with two unicorns because I wanted to keep my friends safe. When I was speaking to the teacher, the two unicorns found a bit of chocolate and some sweets! Also in the room, there were two mermaids talking in the corner as well as doing gymnastics. All of the class were outside because it was lunchtime, but one of the mermaids sprained her ankle because she did a move the wrong way.

Isla Clemie (7)

Kinross Primary School, Kinross

Dear Diary

I went to a funfair and I saw a Pokémon. It was Pikachu! I went to stroke him. Pikachu jumped onto my face and started to lick my face! After what seemed to be forever, Pikachu jumped off my face. Me and Pikachu walked to the nearest ride. It was a roller coaster. Me and Pikachu looked up at the roller coaster. There was an alien! The alien was stuck!

Fraser Younie (7)
Kinross Primary School, Kinross

Dear Diary

Yesterday I went to the zoo but not only did I just go to the zoo, I went to the park and the funfair! Then me and Thea went to the park to have lunch. We were so hungry, we were popping! It was actually a picnic. We then went home because it was getting late.

Today I went horse riding, swimming and had a party! We are tired.

Esther-Joy Lois Johnston (7)

Kinross Primary School, Kinross

Dear Diary

Today I went to a WWE show and I went with a monster. His name is Giggle and he is funny because he always laughs and laughs. When he went to sleep, he snorted like a pig! When we went to the wrestling match, it was fun because we saw a hot dog shop. Well, Giggle was happy because he is in love with hot dogs!

C Jay Duncan (7)
Kinross Primary School, Kinross

Dear Diary

I went to a football match. It was really funny because my favourite player was playing for them with a monster! I tried playing Pokémon Go. I got a milkshake for free because I stole it from the shop! I like playing with my dinosaurs. I like dragons because they are so fun.

Jamie Allan (7)
Kinross Primary School, Kinross

Dear Diary

Today I went to the funfair with my slime and a monster. His name is Bob because he is bald. I went for a picnic and played football. It was as fun as a bouncy castle. Then I went to watch a Kelty Hearts football match. I got a packet of crisps and a drink of Pepsi Max.

Douglas Brown (7)
Kinross Primary School, Kinross

Dear Diary

I went to the zoo with a monster but a gorilla escaped! The gorilla punched the wall and tried to cross the road. People crashed. I was trying to catch it. Finally, it stopped and they caught him and took the gorilla home! It was a weird day.

Angus Younie (7)
Kinross Primary School, Kinross

Dear Diary

Today me and my pet monster went to a funfair. We went on a roller coaster and then it rained. I tripped up and fell into some slime. It was green!
When we got back, I had a shower and me and my monster watched a movie.

Aaron George Yates (7)
Kinross Primary School, Kinross

Dear Diary

Today I went to the park with my best friend, Maia. We saw a tunnel and we went through it and saw a scary dragon behind a big gate! We peeked through and stared at the dragon but in the distance, we saw a whole pack of dragons! When we opened the gate, all of them looked at us. One of the dragons picked us up and said, "Look at them! They are lost dragons." The dragons didn't notice that we were dressed up in dragon clothes!
When it got dark, the dragons noticed that we had dragon clothes on so they locked us in a room that had a tarantula!

Marley Hunter (6)
Lasswade Primary School, Bonnyrigg

Dear Diary

Today I went to gymnastics with my best friend. We did cartwheels, handstands, butterfly stretches and the splits! It was really fun but on the butterfly stretches my best friend cut her knee, which was sad. Next, I went to a gymnastics party and played gymnastics computer games. After we had lunch, we saw a magical unicorn and partied with it! Then we had dinner and had a chocolate milkshake. We got party bags and came home to go to bed. However, I read a book sneakily before bed!

Sophie Marsland (6)

Lasswade Primary School, Bonnyrigg

Dear Diary

One day, I was playing a video game when I accidentally dropped the controller! I suddenly teleported into the game! I teleported into Indigo Quarry! It exploded and covered me in slime. I went to the glass desert and found a spinning dervish slime. When I was flying, I saw a mosaic slime and a tangle slime and a dervish slime too! My mum walked into my room and she saw that I was in the game so I got teleported back home!

Harris McGregor (7)
Lasswade Primary School, Bonnyrigg

Dear Diary

Today I went to Fire Land with a dragon. Its name was Patterns. The colour of it was red, yellow and orange. There was fire everywhere! The fire was not hot so we made a swimming pool with fire in it. We played lots of games called tig and toilet tig. It was really fun. Then it was lunch and we had milk and a pie. Then we went outside again. We played the same game because it was so, so fun.

Brodie Ella Wilson (6)

Lasswade Primary School, Bonnyrigg

Dear Diary

I was walking through the woods and then I saw a unicorn. It was very strange. The sparkly unicorn was lost and the unicorn's tummy was rumbling. It was very hungry. We ate lots of sweets. After, we went to see some bones. Suddenly, the unicorn did magic! I turned into a cow! *Mooo!* Then I turned into a pencil. Then I turned back to normal. Then I was lost in the woods.

Ellie Maxwell (6)
Lasswade Primary School, Bonnyrigg

Dear Diary

Today I went to the seaside and I went with Emma and Chloe. Then a monster came! The monster was huge and the monster was skinny. We got lost and we walked for a long time. We stopped for a break to play with slime. Then we met a unicorn! We all rode the unicorn and we got a potion so we could fly! Then we walked to the funfair. It was fun and jolly and we got a magical goody bag.

Elle Marion Toulouse (6)

Lasswade Primary School, Bonnyrigg

Dear Diary

I was in my room and the magic key was glowing. I held the magic key and it teleported me to a dragon! I climbed onto the dragon. Then the magic key took us to a volcano. A unicorn was there, an evil unicorn! It had jumped out of the volcano. I told my dragon to breathe fire! The unicorn was dead. What an eventful day!

Micheal Dougan (6)
Lasswade Primary School, Bonnyrigg

Dear Diary

Today I met a mermaid called Ava and we went to the park. We were walking to an ice cream shop and then we saw Chloe and Elle. Chloe was wearing a hairband and Elle was wearing a L.O.L. doll dress! Chloe was wearing the same. Then we saw Flo. Flo saw an ice cream van so we ran to it! We had a good day.

Emma Stables (6)
Lasswade Primary School, Bonnyrigg

Dear Diary

Today I went to the funfair. Me and my unicorn had lunch in the tent. I had a strawberry milkshake and Gems, the unicorn, had a baby unicorn! Her name was Ava. She had baby cake. They were happy. The baby unicorn, Ava, was sad and was crying for her mum. The baby was happy when she found her mummy.

Laila Heatlie (6)
Lasswade Primary School, Bonnyrigg

Dear Diary

Today I went to the moon. I saw aliens playing rugby and it was weird. The Irish won and the Scottish team were very angry. Then I went over to the Irish alien team to tell them a secret. They got so excited when they knew my secret! Suddenly, Mum shouted that it was time to go home.

Toby Briggs (6)
Lasswade Primary School, Bonnyrigg

Dear Diary

I went to Minecraft World with a pet dragon. He was in a cave. We went to a Minecraft Star Wars Zoo. When we went to the zoo, we saw a T-rex! It was super big. We climbed on top of the T-rex and ran away. The T-rex was hungry! He had hot dogs and he burped.

Jamie Hamlyn (6)
Lasswade Primary School, Bonnyrigg

Dear Diary

I went to Pokémon Land. It was a mission. I stole all of Alistair's Pokémon. He used all of my Pokémon to battle. I didn't know he had stolen all of my weak Pokémon! I didn't know he had stolen my weak Charizard!

Benjamin Harris (6)

Lasswade Primary School, Bonnyrigg

Dear Diary

I went to the funfair. I went with my grandma. Next, I rode a unicorn and we rode a dragon! Then I had a chocolate milkshake. Then we watched a movie. It was 'How to Train Your Dragon'. At the end, they had three babies. It was so much fun.

Maia Patricia Virgo (7)

Lasswade Primary School, Bonnyrigg

Dear Diary

Today I went to the funfair. I went with a mermaid and I had a chocolate smoothie. It was good! Before we went home I hooked a duck! When I hooked a duck, I won a toy owl and it was pink and yellow! The last one was orange. Then we went home.

Morven Thompson (6)
Lasswade Primary School, Bonnyrigg

Dear Diary

Today I went to the zoo with my best friend and a dragon. Then we got a smoothie and some mint candy sweets. Afterwards, we saw a tall giraffe. She was eating the leaves from the tree. Then I saw a black and white zebra. Then I went home.

Poppy Ann Dunham (6)
Lasswade Primary School, Bonnyrigg

Dear Diary

I went to the park with my friend, Faith. We saw mermaids there! Then we drank slime. We found a unicorn there. It was amazing! Everyone freaked out. "Oh no," someone said. People were screaming because they got frightened.

Simrit Janjua (6)
Lasswade Primary School, Bonnyrigg

Dear Diary

Today I went to a party and had Coke and biscuits. Then I went home and played football. I played on my computer and I had a bar of chocolate. I was with my cousin and he tried to help me with Pokémon on my computer.

Taylor McInnes (6)

Lasswade Primary School, Bonnyrigg

Dear Diary

I went to the funfair and I met an alien and a nice dinosaur. I found treasure and after, we went to the shops. After that, we made slime for a slime party! We were dancing and we played games. After that, we went swimming.

Harris McKenzie (7)

Lasswade Primary School, Bonnyrigg

Dear Diary

Today I went to Sweetie Land with my best friend, The Monster. We went to the gingerbread house and we saw the Gingerbread Man! Oh no. My friend, The Monster, ate him! We had to run and hide. We had great fun!

Rhys Gladstone (7)
Lasswade Primary School, Bonnyrigg

Dear Diary

Today I went to gymnastics with my best friend, the mermaid. We went to the zoo. We went to see the zebras and they galloped and played tig. We went to the cafe for the fluffy cupcakes. What a fantastic day!

Lailah Wilson (6)
Lasswade Primary School, Bonnyrigg

Dear Diary

I went to Art Land. When I got there, I met a tiger. My unicorn played with the tiger. "Roar!" said the tiger.
Me and the tiger and my unicorn played together. My unicorn is yellow and pink.

Faith Barker (6)
Lasswade Primary School, Bonnyrigg

Dear Diary

I went to Superhero Land with my friend.
Our names are Emerson and Leah. Then an
alien spaceship crashed! Chemicals spilt
onto us and we turned into superheroes! We
fought the alien. It was an amazing day.

Emerson Milne (7)

Lasswade Primary School, Bonnyrigg

Dear Diary

Today I went to school with my best friend. We played until the bell went. I went into school and I did Maths. Then we had free play. We went outside and played soldiers. We had an amazing time.

Cameron Smith (6)
Lasswade Primary School, Bonnyrigg

Dear Diary

Today I went to the zoo with a cat. His name is Henry. I saw a Charizard. Charizard is a dragon and a Pokémon. I played with the Charizard. I drank some potions and I ate chocolate!

Eddie Price (7)

Lasswade Primary School, Bonnyrigg

Dear Diary

Today I went on an aeroplane. When I got there, there was chocolate in the sky and candy rain! I saw chocolate grass and a chocolate house. I started to eat. It was delicious.

Mila Dickson (6)

Lasswade Primary School, Bonnyrigg

Dear Diary

I went to school with my best friends, Isla and Maia. We learned how to make a magical fairy and a scary dinosaur out of gooey slime. It was too hard! We had a good time.

Yolanda Lange (6)

Lasswade Primary School, Bonnyrigg

Dear Diary

Today I went to a football lunch party. It was cool! I went with my friend, Monster, and we played football. It was fun and it was one-nil to my team! Then we went home.

Cohen Donoghue (6)
Lasswade Primary School, Bonnyrigg

Dear Diary

I went to the funfair and I went on the Ferris wheel. I went to the bumper cars and I nearly bounced out because it was so bumpy. Then I went home and played Fortnite.

Harry MacGregor (6)

Lasswade Primary School, Bonnyrigg

Dear Diary

Today I went to the zoo and I saw a mermaid. I went with a unicorn and she was beautiful. She ate so many sweets. We saw some monkeys dancing. It was so much fun.

Keeley McKenna (6)
Lasswade Primary School, Bonnyrigg

Dear Diary

Today I went to the funfair with my best friend. We went on the Ferris wheel. It went high in the sky. We ate a cheese sandwich. I felt happy and it was amazing!

Carter Dewar (6)
Lasswade Primary School, Bonnyrigg

Dear Diary

Today I went to the zoo with my friend, the swan. We ate chocolate ice cream and drank fizzy juice. Then we played tig! I felt happy because we had great fun.

Zaynab Wahid (6)

Lasswade Primary School, Bonnyrigg

Dear Diary

Today I went to school with my family and unicorn. We played tig with my best friend. We had great fun! Then we had sweets. They were really yummy.

Aaliyah Milliken (6)
Lasswade Primary School, Bonnyrigg

Dear Diary

I went to football. I got injured but I didn't cry. I was brave! My mum and dad came because they had finished work. Then I won four-two!

Riley Henry (6)
Lasswade Primary School, Bonnyrigg

Dear Diary

Today I went to the funfair. I went with a unicorn. I met a mermaid and we went to a cafe to have a drink. Then we went to gymnastics.

Megan Murphy (7)
Lasswade Primary School, Bonnyrigg

Dear Diary

I went to the zoo with Brooke. On the way, we met Riley. We fed the sharks. It was fun! We also met a dog. It was sunny and a hot day. It was getting dark so we had to go home.

The next day, we went to school. It was boring. After that, we went to the park. We played tig. Then we went to my house. We played outside and then Brooke and Riley had to go home.

Emily Grace Williamson (7)
Milton Of Leys Primary School, Milton Of Leys

Dear Diary

My name is Brooklyn and this is my diary.
I went to the park with Emily, Shonnie,
Rosana and Leo. We played tig and I was it.
Then when Shonnie went home, me, Rosana
and Emily begged for a sleepover. We got
one! We stayed up all night and had a
midnight feast.
The next day, we went swimming.

Brooke McMillan (7)
Milton Of Leys Primary School, Milton Of Leys

Dear Diary

It was raining. Waves were crashing. I was all wet and I could hear the thunder roaring. I could taste the salty seawater. I saw thousands of Scots waiting for us to battle. I was furious but a little bit excited. I jumped out of the longboat and swam to the shore on my back. I started the battle! I had cuts on my arm. There was blood but I kept battling. I used my axe to chop their heads and legs off! I saw blood on the ground. I saw dead bodies lying on the ground. We ran to the longboat quickly so the Scots didn't jump on it and break the boat. Lots of the Scots and my Viking friends were killed. We all went back to Scandinavia. I felt a bit sad but happy.

Michalina Slusarek (7)
St Pius X RC Primary School, Dundee

Dear Diary

I was on the longboat with rain falling heavily and high waves crashing on the longboat. The thunder was roaring, making strong winds and I could taste salty water running down my throat. When I looked up, I saw hundreds of Scots waiting. I felt a bit seasick at the time and scared, but I felt really excited for the battle! I jumped off the longboat and swam to shore. I swung my axe over my head and chopped seven Scots' heads off! I saw lots of disgusting blood. I felt so sick. I heard lots of shouts for help. After that, I felt metal come across my arm! I saw that a Scot had cut my arm! I was roaring with pain. I felt very angry. I could see dead bodies everywhere. I was running all the way back to the longboat and I climbed up to get on with the other Vikings coming with me. I started rowing with all my strength and was going all the way back to Scandinavia! I was relieved because I was alive.

Daniel Cecil (7)
St Pius X RC Primary School, Dundee

Dear Diary

I was on a longship. Tidal waves crashed on the ship. Flashing thunder struck the ship. Salty water was in my mouth. It was midnight. The ship was flooded with water. Rain was falling. There were shiny, sparkly stars. I saw lots of Scots ready for battle. I was furious and jealous and horrified! I jumped off the ship and swam to shore. I killed a man. I swung my axe on someone's neck and chopped their head off. There was blood. I felt furious! Someone hurt me but I didn't care. I saw hammers charging at me but I dodged them. I was really furious. I heard swords. I smelt blood and it made me sick. I swung my axe and chopped lots of people's legs off. I saw dead bodies everywhere. I quickly swam to the boat, then climbed the giant side. Some of my pals survived!

We sailed back to Scandinavia. I was glad, relieved and relaxed with joy.

Max Adam (7)

St Pius X RC Primary School, Dundee

Dear Diary

There was strong, heavy wind and there was heavy rain. Waves were roaring strongly. Thunder and lightning were crashing everywhere. Dark clouds were in the sky. There were Scots waiting for me! I tasted salty water. I felt excited and nervous. I was soaking. I jumped to the beach. I was swinging my axe and I chopped off a lot of heads and legs. There was blood. I heard Scots and Vikings screaming. I felt furious! I saw dead bodies and blood. I swam to the longboat and climbed up the side and we rode back to where I live. I feel good because I survived.

Gabriela Lesiecka (7)
St Pius X RC Primary School, Dundee

Dear Diary

Tonight was parents' night in the gym hall. It was good. Mrs Glancy said I was having a good week. I was doing all my work and having brain breaks. Nan said, "I'll get you something big - a new scooter!"
When we went home, Nan got me a new scooter! Grandad said, "I'll get you a new dirt bike!"
I was given surprises. It was cool and I felt good!

Kevin Souter (9)
St Pius X RC Primary School, Dundee

Dear Diary

One time, there was a magical creature called The Sweet Cherry. Her magic was terrible because she wasn't careful. I took her to a doctor of magic to help with this problem. The doctor said to practise her magic and then he came to help her with the problem. The doctor told her that it wasn't hard but she tried and it didn't work. "You just need to calm down," said the doctor of magic. She tried again and it worked.

"Thank you!" said the unicorn.

"You are welcome!" said the doctor. We were happy.

Laura Kacala (6)

St Thomas' Primary School, Riddrie

Dear Diary

Yesterday I went to the awesome zoo and saw the fierce, dangerous lions. Next, I saw the huge elephant stomp across the sticky mud. Then I touched a cute, soft bunny. After a while, we had lunch and it was delicious! I had sandwiches, cookies, apples, grapes and a drink. After lunch, I got a lovely chocolate ice cream and it was amazing. Birds kept licking it! Next, there were giraffes and they had the longest necks ever! They ate green, juicy leaves. Finally, I got in my clean car to go home. I can't wait for next time.

Findlay Smith (7)
St Thomas' Primary School, Riddrie

Dear Diary

I'm going to write about my school day. First, I woke up. I got ready and walked to school with my mum. I saw my friend. Next, I played games with them and it was amazing. My favourite was princesses and fairies! Then it was lunch and I had a chicken burger with salad, fruit and water. After that, it was learning time because we need to learn. We were learning rounding numbers and it was amazingly fun! Last but not least, when I was coming home from school, my baby cousin and my mum came to pick me up and it was fun!

Haifa Minhas (7)
St Thomas' Primary School, Riddrie

Dear Diary

The other day, I was coming home from school. I was watching my iPad and fell asleep. I had a dream about Unicorn Land and I met a unicorn. It said, "Ride me!" So I rode it and it ran and ran until it stopped. "Touch me!" So I did. It felt as fluffy as a dog's fur. In fact, even fluffier than a dog's fur! Then it ran as fast as it could to take me somewhere amazing. As if I hadn't seen enough! Then I woke up.
"Unicorn!" I said loudly. It was all just a dream!

Hayley-Jay Johnston (7)
St Thomas' Primary School, Riddrie

Dear Diary

Last year I went to Benidorm and it was roasting hot. First, when I got off the plane, I went straight into the water, but it was cool because the water was in the shade. Next, I went to the hotel. People were very nice. After that, I went to get tasty food and it was so yummy. Then I went to a place where there were activities you could do. After that, it was late so I went to the cosiest bed I've ever been in. After midnight, it was the morning so it was time to go. I made a fuss about going home.

Jessica Reilly (7)
St Thomas' Primary School, Riddrie

Dear Diary

I am writing to tell you about my day at the funfair. It all started when me and my family said, "What should we do?"
I said, "Let's go to the funfair!"
My family said, "Yes!" So we went to the funfair.
When we got there, straight away I said I wanted to go to the funny mirror. My brother said, "I want to go to the helter-skelter!"
Both of us got our pick and went on the things we wanted to.

Lewis Murray (7)
St Thomas' Primary School, Riddrie

Dear Diary

One day, I went to the unicorn park and I found a friend. I asked her if I could play and she said yes. We went to play on the swings. Then we were really hungry so we got a burger and chips. We asked our mum if we could have a play date. Our mum said yes and we were allowed! We were so excited. Instead of a play date, we had a sleepover. It was so much fun!

Hollie Sneddon (7)
St Thomas' Primary School, Riddrie

Dear Diary

Ten people were playing football and I scored a hat-trick! Then a yellow Minion came along called Kevin. We were both brilliant at scoring. It was a good day! Kevin became my best friend and we play football all the time. Something we get called is the Dynamic Duo! One day, when we are older, we will play for Celtic. I promise.

Harlyn Jenkins (7)
St Thomas' Primary School, Riddrie

Dear Diary

I went to a magical place called the Unicorn Kingdom. I went with my unicorn friend, my bunny friend, my best friend, Zoe, and my family. There was a big park and there was an ice skating park! We had a blast. Then I remembered that I had forgotten my monster friend so we all went to get him. We were happy.

Taylor-Anne Shreenan (7)
St Thomas' Primary School, Riddrie

Dear Diary

It was a beautiful sunny day. We went with the family to the park. There were many children. Mom was resting with my younger brother on the bench. There was a huge slide in the park. I was playing with my dad. We spent a fun day with the whole family!

Gabriela Skolarczyk (6)

St Thomas' Primary School, Riddrie

Dear Diary

This was a terrible day at first. I got a note from the chickens. The note said: 'We're going on holiday. From the chickens'. I thought to myself, *but I only have a few eggs left!* They weren't enough for everyone that would need Easter eggs! All of a sudden, I heard a knock on the door. I was swarmed by all of the animals I was warned about! I said no and then yes and let them in. Then me and the animals all saved Easter!

Oliver Parker (7)
St Thomas' RC Primary School, Arbroath

Dear Diary

This was a hard day because all of the chickens went on holiday. The chickens went away so I had to do all of the work. I heard a loud noise and saw the foxes, the geese and the badgers! I was not scared and let them inside. The geese laid more eggs! The foxes made paintbrushes with their tails! The badgers dug from the ground. We all saved Easter!

Nina Kosznik (7) & Lola Susan Heenan (6)

St Thomas' RC Primary School, Arbroath

Dear Diary

This was a bad day for me. I had to send some letters to get help. Next, my doorbell rang and I saw some Easter Bunnies! I was scared. Then I gave them some colours and paintbrushes to help me paint some Easter eggs. They saved Easter! I delivered all the eggs at the park.

Connor Falconer (7)

St Thomas' RC Primary School, Arbroath

Dear Diary

This was the most terrible Easter in my life. My chickens were on holiday! What could I do with no chickens? I couldn't make any egg hunts! Then the badgers, sly foxes and geese came and saved Easter! They made the eggs and painted the eggs to help me.

Marty Emery (6)
St Thomas' RC Primary School, Arbroath

Dear Diary

This had been a terrible day at my Easter Bunny house. All of my workers left! At last, I heard my doorbell ring. I opened the door. It was the foxes to help me! I was right. The foxes did help me save Easter!

Luca Cassidy (7)

St Thomas' RC Primary School, Arbroath

Dear Diary

Yesterday I went to my gran's birthday party. The time was 11:30 and we gave her a big, creamy, delicious, scrumptious carrot cake. We gave her presents and she loved them. Just then, the cake fell on top of my gran! She was very sad. I went down to the bakery and tried to find a carrot cake but there wasn't any left. I had to go to the other bakery on the other side of the town. I needed to get in my mum's car. My mum drove me there. I rushed in the door and got the cake!

Emily Elizabeth Doctor (7)

Woodlands Primary School, Cumbernauld

Dear Diary

Yesterday, on Saturday morning at 10am, I went to the zoo with my best friend. I was so excited! So was my best friend.
When we arrived at the zoo, we went to see the horses, but I saw a unicorn! At first, I thought it was my imagination but it wasn't. It was real! When I went to pet it, me and my friend teleported to a magical place! The unicorn was with us. We could talk to the unicorn somehow. I said to the unicorn, "Where are we?"
It replied, saying, "We are in a magical land and for you to get out, you need to get to the palace!"
So we walked and walked. When we were one mile away from the palace, we had a break and sat down. We were very tired. An hour later, we started walking again. Finally, we got to the palace! The unicorn was there. He said, "Finally, you two are here! You may go back to the zoo now, bye-bye!"

We were then sent back to the zoo!

I said, "I wonder why that unicorn was here?"

"Me too!" said my friend.

It was late at night so we went home. It took us an hour to get home.

Lola McLean (8)

Woodlands Primary School, Cumbernauld

Dear Diary

On Saturday, me and my family and friends went to the park for three hours. Then we went to my house for lunch. Then we went to the funfair! For a snack, I got sweets. I had a pet dog and I still do. It was my pet dog's birthday. She was at the funfair. We went on a lot of rides. It was super fun! After that, my dad stayed at home with my dog and we went to the shops. We went to Costa. I got a milkshake. It was super yummy.

At the toyshop, I got slime! I played with it on the way to the zoo.

When I got in the zoo, I FaceTimed my dad to see how my dog was. Then it came up that there was no answer! My dad always answers because he loves when people FaceTime him. I got out of the car. The zoo looked super nice. There were a load of animals! All of a sudden, all the animals got out of their cage! I said, "What happened?"

Then a sheep got away! I said, "What have I done?"

The zookeeper said, "Nothing!"

I said, "Who did it then?"

"No one did it!"

"I am so sorry if I scared them!"

Poppy Millar (7)

Woodlands Primary School, Cumbernauld

Dear Diary

Yesterday, at three o'clock, me and my friend went to the park. We had so much fun, but something appeared in the middle of the park. It was a Poké Ball! I said, "What is that in the middle of the park?"
My friend said, "I don't know!"

Then the Poké Ball was opening! A Pokémon appeared! It was a Pokémon called Pikachu. Then he became my partner and my friend's partner. Me and my partner and my friend were happy.

Sonny Sandhu (7)

Woodlands Primary School, Cumbernauld

Dear Diary

Today me and my friend went to Adventure Planet. It was 12:30pm when we arrived. We played for an hour, up and down the ball pit and the slides! After, we went down for food and a drink.

When we went back to the slide, a boy was blocking us so we couldn't go down it! When the workers kicked the boy out, we went back to the slide to play. After the hour, my friend came to my house for two hours and thirty seconds. Then she went home and I fell asleep.

Lilly McLay (7)

Woodlands Primary School, Cumbernauld

Dear Diary

One day, I saw a unicorn and a mermaid! I screamed loudly. The unicorn strode to me. I gave it candyfloss. Then a mermaid peered out of the water. I ran to the mermaid princess. I said, "Who are you?"
The mermaid said, "I'm Jordan." I love mermaids.
"I wish you could come out of the water but you can't!" The unicorn fell asleep and Jordan did too.

Isla (7)
Woodlands Primary School, Cumbernauld

Dear Diary

On Friday afternoon I went to the funfair. There were lots of rides! I went to the funhouse first. After that, I went on the Ferris wheel. When I got on the Ferris wheel, the wheel snapped! Then it started to roll. It squashed cars and people! When my cube hit the ground, I jumped out! The wheel went the opposite way to my house so I went home and had a Domino's. I enjoyed it.

Tyler Rolland (7)
Woodlands Primary School, Cumbernauld

Dear Diary

One day, I went to the shops and my mum gave me a pound for a claw machine. I won Candy Cat and Susie Sheep! We went home and put the toys away and then we went to swimming class.

When we got back home, Candy Cat had shrunk! Then I realised, since I was only four, it could be four like me. I felt happy. Then we went to have lunch. We played and we had so much fun that day!

Lily-Anne Elizabeth Fraser (7)

Woodlands Primary School, Cumbernauld

Dear Diary

Me and my friends were going to the school disco. We got there. There was no one there. It was completely silent. "I'm scared," said Amelia. "It's haunted!"
We tried to get out of there. The school door slammed! I could hear a shadow running across! We ran and ran and ran for days and days.
Now I think the shadow has gone, but has it?

Nathan Andrew Snedden (7)
Woodlands Primary School, Cumbernauld

Dear Diary

Yesterday I went to the cinema with my friends. We had popcorn. It was delicious. Then we got a drink. I got apple juice. Then the film was done. We went to Domino's and got a pepperoni pizza. After I ate my pizza, I went home and put my pyjamas on and went to bed happy.

Alannah Dyce (7)
Woodlands Primary School, Cumbernauld

Dear Diary

One day, I went to the zoo with Pikachu the Pokémon. The lion roared so loud! We saw ants bringing a leaf to a rope. Then it was lunchtime. Then we saw an Arctic wolf. I went home, had dinner and went to bed.

Noah Meppem (7)
Woodlands Primary School, Cumbernauld

 YoungWriters® Est. 1991

Young Writers Information

We hope you have enjoyed reading this book – and that you will continue to in the coming years.

If you're a young writer who enjoys reading and creative writing, or the parent of an enthusiastic poet or story writer, do visit our website **www.youngwriters.co.uk**. Here you will find free competitions, workshops and games, as well as recommended reads, a poetry glossary and our blog. There's lots to keep budding writers motivated to write!

If you would like to order further copies of this book, or any of our other titles, then please give us a call or order via your online account.

Young Writers
Remus House
Coltsfoot Drive
Peterborough
PE2 9BF
(01733) 890066
info@youngwriters.co.uk

Join in the conversation!
Tips, news, giveaways and much more!

 YoungWritersUK

 @YoungWritersCW